the JUMBLIES

by Edward Lear

TOP THAT

Licensed exclusively to Top That Publishing Ltd
Tide Mill Way, Woodbridge, Suffolk, IP12 1AP, UK
www.topthatpublishing.com
Copyright © 2013 Tide Mill Media
All rights reserved
0 2 4 6 8 9 7 5 3 1
Manufactured in China

Illustrated by Sam McPhillips
Written by Edward Lear

ISBN 978-1-78244-213-4

A catalogue record for this book is available from the British Library

'For my Mum and Dad, Silkiesue and Robert too x'
Sam McPhillips

They went to sea in a sieve, they did,
In a sieve they went to sea:
In spite of all their friends could say,
On a winter's morn, on a stormy day,
In a sieve they went to sea!

And when the sieve turned round and round,
And everyone cried, 'You'll all be drowned!'
They called aloud, 'Our sieve ain't big,
But we don't care a button! We don't care a fig!
In a sieve we'll go to sea!'

Far and few, far and few,
  Are the lands where the Jumblies live;
Their heads are green, and their hands are blue,
  And they went to sea in a sieve.

They sailed away in a sieve, they did,
In a sieve they sailed so fast,
With only a beautiful pea-green veil
Tied with a ribbon by way of a sail,
To a small tobacco-pipe mast;

And everyone said, who saw them go,
'O won't they soon be upset, you know!
For the sky is dark, and the voyage is long,
And happen what may, it's extremely wrong
In a sieve to sail so fast!'

Far and few, far and few,
Are the lands where the Jumblies live;
Their heads are green, and their hands are blue,
And they went to sea in a sieve.

The water it soon came in, it did,
The water it soon came in.
So to keep them dry, they wrapped their feet
In a pinky paper all folded neat,
And they fastened it down with a pin.

And they passed the night in a crockery jar,
And each of them said, 'How wise we are!
Though the sky be dark, and the voyage be long,
Yet we never can think we were rash or wrong,
While round in our sieve we spin!'

Far and few, far and few,
Are the lands where the Jumblies live;

Their heads are green, and their hands are blue,
And they went to sea in a sieve.

And all night long they sailed away;
And when the sun went down,
They whistled and warbled a moony song
To the echoing sound of a coppery gong,
In the shade of the mountains brown.

Far and few, far and few,
Are the lands where the Jumblies live;

'O Timballo! How happy we are,
When we live in a sieve and a crockery jar,
And all night long in the moonlight pale,
We sail away with a pea-green sail,
In the shade of the mountains brown!'

Their heads are green, and their hands are blue,
And they went to sea in a sieve.

They sailed to the Western Sea, they did,
To a land all covered in trees,
And they bought an owl, and a useful cart,
And a pound of rice, and a cranberry tart,
And a hive of silvery bees.
And they bought a pig, and some green jackdaws,
And a lovely monkey with lollipop paws,
And forty bottles of Ring-Bo-Ree,
And no end of Stilton cheese.

Far and few, far and few,
Are the lands where the Jumblies live;
Their heads are green, and their hands are blue,
And they went to sea in a sieve.

And in twenty years they all came back,
In twenty years or more,
And everyone said, 'How tall they've grown!
For they've been to the Lakes, and the Torrible Zone,
And the hills of the Chankly Bore!'

And they drank their health, and gave them a feast
Of dumplings made of beautiful yeast;
And everyone said, 'If we only live,
We too will go to sea in a sieve,
To the hills of the Chankly Bore!'

Far and few, far and few,
Are the lands where the Jumblies live,
Their heads are green, and their hands are blue,
And they went to sea in a sieve.